Big Bear, Spare That Tree

by Richard J. Margolis
pictures by Jack Kent

SCHOLASTIC BOOK SERVICES
NEW YORK • TORONTO • LONDON • AUCKLAND • SYDNEY • TOKYO

ISBN 0-590-31714-8

12 11 10 9 8 7 6 5 4 3 2 1   3   2 3 4 5 6/8

Printed in the U.S.A.   07

In memory of Gram,

defender of many nests

–R.J.M.

Big Bear was chopping down
an oak tree for firewood.
Whack!
His sharp ax
bit deep into the tree.

As Big Bear chopped,

he sang,

"My arms are strong,

my ax is long.

I like to chop,

I'll never ... I'll never ..."

"Stop!"

said a voice from above.

"Huh?" said Big Bear,

squinting at the sky.

But he did not see anyone.

Whack! Whack!

Big Bear went back to work.

He sang,

"My arms are long,

my ax is strong.

I must admit

I'd hate to ... hate to ..."

"Quit! Quit!"

said the voice from above.

Big Bear looked up again.

This time he saw a nest.

It was held

between two branches

halfway up the tall oak.

In the nest sat a blue jay.

She was staring

straight at Big Bear.

"Quit your chopping, Big Bear,"

Blue Jay commanded.

"Stop it at once."

Big Bear frowned.

"You shouldn't be up there,

Blue Jay," he said politely.

"It's not safe."

Blue Jay beat her wings,
but she did not fly away.

"Moving is out of the question,"
she said.
"I'm sitting on three eggs.
When they hatch—
and they will hatch
very soon now—
I shall be the mother
of three baby blue jays."

Big Bear turned away.
"I'll believe that
when I see it,"
he said.

"You won't see it
    if you don't believe it,"
she replied.
"Chopping and hatching
    don't mix."

Big Bear tightened his grip
on the ax.
"I need fuel for my cabin,"
he growled.

Blue Jay glared down
at Big Bear.
"I need shelter for my eggs,"
she cried.

"This tree belongs to me,"
he shouted.
"But I live here!"
Blue Jay shouted back.

Whack! Whack! Whack!

Big Bear started chopping again.

The gash in the tree

was getting deeper and deeper.

"My cabin's cold,

my ax is bold,"

sang Big Bear.

"It's getting late,

I must not . . . must not . . ."

"Wait! Wait! Wait!"

called Blue Jay.

Big Bear sighed.

"What is it this time,

Blue Jay?"

"I have made up a song
just for you," she said.

"It has a message."

"Will I like it?" Big Bear asked.

"You'll love it," she promised.

Blue Jay sang
in a scratchy voice.
"Rock-a-bye, babies,
still in their yolk.
When the ax falls,
so will the oak."
"I don't like it," said Big Bear.
He got ready to swing his ax.

"There's more, there's more,"
Blue Jay said quickly.
She leaned over the nest
and sang at the top
of her voice.
"Rock-a-bye, blue jays,
high in the air.
When the tree falls,
it could fall on Big Bear."

Big Bear's face got very dark.
"Are you finished?" he asked.

Blue Jay looked at her three eggs.
"I guess we are finished," she said.

Whack! Whack! Whack! Whack!

Big Bear's ax struck the tree

again and again.

Splinters flew in all directions.

"From what I've seen,

my ax is keen,"

he sang as he chopped.

"It's only fair,

I am...I am...I am..."

"Big Bear,"

Blue Jay whispered.

"Something is happening up here."

Big Bear did not look up.

He did not stop chopping.

"I can't hear you, Blue Jay,"

he said.

Blue Jay spoke in a louder whisper.

"I said something is happening.

Something is moving under me."

"Uh huh," said Big Bear. "That's nice."

Whack! Whack! Whack!

Whack!

Whack!

Now Blue Jay stood on her head
inside the nest.
When she spoke,
her voice sounded very far away.

First she said, "It may be."

Then she said,
"It might be."

A little later she said, "It could be."

And after
a moment
she shouted,
"IT IS."

Blue Jay flew out of the nest.
She circled the tree four times.
She swooped, dipped, and
landed on Big Bear's shoulder.
He was still chopping.
"Look up, Big Bear, look up,"
she yelled in Big Bear's ear.

Big Bear turned
to stare at Blue Jay.
He rubbed his ear.
He looked up.

What he saw, poking over

the top of the nest,

were three small beaks.

Big Bear was so surprised,

he dropped his ax.

Then he smiled.

"Gosh," he said,

"they really are baby blue jays."

Big Bear waved a paw
at the babies.
"Hello," he said.
"Hello, blue jays."
"Chirp chirp chirp," they said.

Just then the tall oak
made a loud, creaky noise.
The trunk trembled.
The top of the tree
began to sway.
"Oh dear," said Big Bear.
"I think the tree is coming down."

"My babies! My babies!"
screamed Blue Jay,
flying up to the nest.
"Don't just stand there, Big Bear.
Do something."

Big Bear looked at the tree.

It was starting to fall.

"Well," he said,

"I guess I can try."

He wrapped his big arms

around the tree.

With all his strength

he pushed against it.

"Ugh," Big Bear grunted.

"Holding up a tree is hard work."

Blue Jay flew down
and stood on Big Bear's head.
"You are doing fine, Big Bear,"
she said.
"Now just back up a little
and start letting the tree down
nice and easy."
Big Bear did as he was told.
He backed up slowly,
letting the tree down inch by inch.
He was breathing hard.
"Steady there," said Blue Jay.

"I don't think I can last
much longer," Big Bear gasped.
"It's getting heavier and heavier."

Blue Jay did not answer.

She was looking at the nest

and her babies.

"Blue Jay," said Big Bear
a few steps later.
"What is it, Big Bear?"
"My arms are hurting, Blue Jay.
I think I am going
to drop the tree."

"No, Big Bear," said Blue Jay.

"You are not going

to drop the tree."

"It is very nice of you

to say that," muttered Big Bear.

Suddenly it was all over.
Big Bear backed up
two more steps.
He was holding
the tree's topmost branch.
Very carefully,
he let the tall oak
settle on the grass.

"You did it. You did it,"
cried Blue Jay,
hopping up and down.
"I did it," panted Big Bear,
sitting on the fallen tree.
"Chirp chirp chirp,"
said the baby blue jays,
still in their nest.

When Big Bear
caught his breath,
he picked up the nest
and gently placed it
over his cabin door.
"They will be safer up here,"
he said to Blue Jay,
"away from dogs and cats."

Then Big Bear raised his ax.

Whack!

He started splitting the tree

for firewood.

Blue Jay flew into the nest
with her babies
and began to sing.
"Rock-a-bye, Big Bear,
our last-minute friend.
He was mean at the start
and kind in..."
Blue Jay paused
and flapped her wings.
"Now what rhymes
with friend?" she asked.

Big Bear laughed.

"That's easy,"

he said as he chopped.

"The end. The end.

The end."

RICHARD J. MARGOLIS's lighthearted stories for beginning readers include two about Big Bear, *Wish Again, Big Bear* (a Junior Literary Guild selection) and *Big Bear to the Rescue* (a Greenwillow Read-alone Book). He is the author of two books of poetry, *Only the Moon and Me* and *Looking for a Place,* as well as several other prose works.

Mr. Margolis and his wife, Diane Rothbard Margolis, live in Georgetown, Connecticut.

JACK KENT has had more than fifty books for children published since 1968 when his first book, *Just Only John,* came out. Among the very popular books he has both written and illustrated are *Fat Cat, There's No Such Thing as a Dragon,* and *Hoddy Doddy* (a Greenwillow Read-alone Book). The comic strip *King Aroo* was a creation of Mr. Kent's that brought him recognition as a highly talented cartoonist.

Jack Kent and his wife live in San Antonio, Texas. They have one son, Jack.